To Neil &
Eleanor,
Remember Mommy will
always love you!

MW00908009

Sometimes Mommy is Anxious
A little book about BIG feelings

Written by **Marci Chapman** and **Lindsay Croce**

Illustrations by Yana Karpenko

© 2022 Marci Chapman and Lindsay Croce. All rights reserved.

No part of this book may be reproduced, stored in a retrieval system, or transmitted by any means without the written permission of the author.

AuthorHouse™
1663 Liberty Drive
Bloomington, IN 47403
www.authorhouse.com
Phone: 833-262-8899

Because of the dynamic nature of the Internet, any web addresses or links contained in this book may have changed since publication and may no longer be valid. The views expressed in this work are solely those of the author and do not necessarily reflect the views of the publisher, and the publisher hereby disclaims any responsibility for them.

Any people depicted in stock imagery provided by Getty Images are models, and such images are being used for illustrative purposes only. Certain stock imagery © Getty Images.

This book is printed on acid-free paper.

ISBN: 978-1-6655-5105-2 (sc)
978-1-6655-5107-6 (hc)
978-1-6655-5106-9 (e)

Library of Congress Control Number: 2022902253

Print information available on the last page.

Published by AuthorHouse 02/17/2022

authorHOUSE®

Dedication

Dedicated to our loving families,
especially our amazing husbands, Remo and Michael,
and our beautiful children, Audrey, Michael, Remo, and Van.

Sometimes Mommy may be full of tears,
but trust me, there is no need to fear.

It's okay, Mommy will always love you.

3

Sometimes staying home all day is tough, but don't worry, you are always enough.

4

It's okay, Mommy will always love you.

Sometimes having a little help
from the best can give Mommy
some much needed rest.

6

It's okay, Mommy will always love you.

Sometimes Mommy only wants to scrub
and clean, but I promise that you are seen.

It's okay, Mommy will always love you.

Sometimes when you're up to no good,
Mommy may not react the way she should.

10

It's okay, Mommy will always love you.

Sometimes Mommy doesn't want to go outside,
even when there isn't a single cloud in the sky.

It's okay,
Mommy will always love you.

Sometimes
Mommy needs
a mental break,
but she'll
be back, for
goodness sake.

14

It's okay, Mommy will always love you.

Sometimes Mommy may breathe real, real fast, but I promise you, it won't last.

It's okay, Mommy will always love you.

Sometimes Mommy has reached her limit,
don't be upset, just give her a minute.

It's okay, Mommy will always love you.

Sometimes you may feel all alone,
while Mommy sits and stares at her phone.

20

It's okay, Mommy will always love you.

Sometimes Mommy may seem sleepy all day,
while you sing, dance, and play away.

It's okay, Mommy will always love you.

Sometimes the worried look on Mommy's face can be fixed by your warm embrace.

It's okay, Mommy will always love you.

So when Mommy gets anxious, what do you do?
Just love your Mommy and NEVER EVER EVER stop being YOU.
Mommy loves you!

Printed in the United States
by Baker & Taylor Publisher Services